The Boy Who Cried Wolf

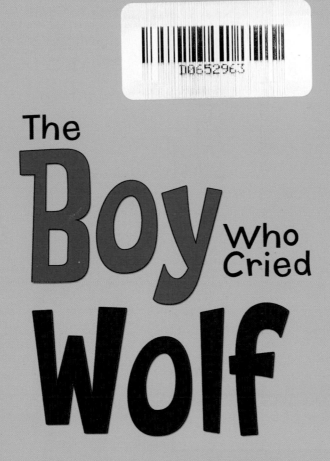

An Aesop's Fable retold by Eric Blair

Illustrated by Dianne Silverman

www.raintreepublishers.co.uk
Visit our website to find out
more information about
Raintree books.

To order:
☎ Phone 0845 6044371
🖷 Fax +44 (0) 1865 312263
🖳 Email myorders@raintreepublishers.co.uk

Customers from outside the UK please telephone +44 1865 312262

Raintree is an imprint of Capstone Global Library Limited,
a company incorporated in England and Wales having its registered office
at 7 Pilgrim Street, London, EC4V 6LB
– Registered company number: 6695582

Art Director: Kay Fraser
Graphic Designers: Emily Harris and Victoria Allen
Production Specialist: Michelle Biedschied
Editor: Catherine Veitch
Originated by Capstone Global Library Ltd
Printed and bound in China by Leo Paper Products Ltd

ISBN 978 1 406 24297 3 (paperback)
16 15 14 13 12
10 9 8 7 6 5 4 3 2 1

British Library Cataloguing in Publication Data
A full catalogue record for this book is available
from the British Library.

What is a fable?
A fable is a story that teaches a lesson.
In some fables, animals may talk and
act the way people do. A Greek slave
named Aesop created some of the world's
favourite fables. Aesop's Fables have been
enjoyed for more than 2,000 years.

What happened next?

Read the story to
find out...

Once upon a time, there was a young shepherd boy.

Every morning, the boy led his father's sheep to an open field. There, the sheep grazed on the grass.

The boy stayed in the field with
the sheep all day long.

One day, the boy was bored. He decided to play a joke on the villagers.

He ran to the village and cried, "Wolf!
Help! There is a wolf attacking my sheep!"

The villagers were kind. They left their work
and came running to the field to chase
the wolf away.

11

But it was a trick.

The sheep were fine. They were happily eating. There was no wolf.

14

The boy laughed. It was so easy to fool the villagers!

The boy played the same trick again
and again.

Each time, the villagers came running.
Each time, there was no wolf.

One day, wolves really did attack the boy's sheep.

The boy was scared. He ran to the village and screamed, "Help! Wolves are attacking my sheep!"

But no one listened to the boy.
No one came to help.

The villagers did not trust the boy,
and the wolves ate his sheep.

Because the boy had lied so many times, nobody believed him, even when he was telling the truth.

The End